Mortimer and Me:
The
BIGFOOT MYSTERY

by Kathie McMahon

illustrated by Tom Tate

D1411473

Pearl White Books

Text copyright © 2020 by Kathie McMahon
Cover and Illustration copyright © 2020 by Tom Tate

Published by Pearl White Books, an imprint of DK Affiliates, LLC
PO Box 2572
Gilbert, AZ 85299

Printed in the United States of America.

ISBN: 978-0-578-68593-9

*For all those
who believe in things
they can't see.*

TRAILBLAZER JOURNAL

Chapters:

Chapter 1
Camping with the Trailblazers

"**W**hy couldn't Muffin come with us?" whines Lily. She leans back into the camping chair and flops her arms down in defeat. "Jimmy got to bring Mortimer."

Mom sighs as she unloads the sleeping bags from the van. "Sweetie, a cat and a camping trip are not a good combination."

"Yeah, Muffin would make perfect bait for a bear." I try to keep my balance with outstretched arms as I walk on top of a fallen tree trunk. I take a final leap to the ground and throw up my arms in victory, like I had just completed the balance beam in the Olympics. "And for your information, I didn't bring Mortimer. He does live in the forest, you know."

"Come on, you guys," Dad says, as he bends over to pound in a stake. "Let's get this tent up before dark. Mortimer is doing his part."

I giggle at the sight of Mortimer, a big clumsy moose who is trying to help - as usual. Our family's tent covers most of his body as he holds up the center on his huge antlers.

Lily wails even more. "Why can't we have a pop-up like Keiko's family?"

Dad stands up and grimaces as

he holds his back. "Because firefighters don't make as much money as computer programmers. Besides, it makes earning the Outdoor Adventure badge much more meaningful when you have to rough it. Come on, let's get cracking, kids."

I glance over at the camping space next to us, where the Tang family's pop-up trailer is already set up. Justin and I have been best friends ever since the soccer game between the teachers and the third graders. Dad and Mr. Tang decided to form a scouting group called the Trailblazers, which includes seven kids from our third grade class. Besides me and Justin, there's Terrance, Brian, Chelsey, Brittany, and Allison. We get to do all this cool stuff and earn badges. Dad just finished helping us earn our Emergency

9-1-1 badges, where we got to visit the fire station and train just like real firefighters. Now our families are here on this camping trip during Memorial Day weekend to earn our Outdoor Adventure badge.

I wave to Justin, who is helping his dad put up a tarp for a covered outdoor area in front of their trailer. Then I scoot over to our tent to help Dad.

Lily is still grumbling about her dumb cat. Mom leads her over to help set up the cooking utensils at the campfire. "I'm sure Charlie is taking good care of Muffin, who is much happier staying with him next door, I promise. Now come and be my cooking assistant."

"Can I be your sous chef, like on Chopped Junior?" Lily starts to bounce up and down.

Mom pinches her eyebrows together. "I don't know how you're even familiar with that term, but one thing is for certain - you watch way too much TV."

I crawl under the tent and come face to face with Mortimer's softball-sized knees. His enormous body is too big to fit inside the tent, so his rear end sticks out the entry flap. Only his tail moves back and forth to flick away the flies. He stands perfectly still while balancing the center of the tent on his antlers. He seems happy to finally be of some help, unlike some of his other attempts. I smile as I remember the time he tried to help out at Charlie's Market and ended up knocking cans off the shelves and crunching the cereal on the floor.

"Jimmy, come and hold the stakes

for me. It'll go much faster if I don't have to keep them in my mouth as I hammer." Dad peeks under the tent. "And don't cause Mortimer to move a muscle. He's been a great help today."

I slide under the tent to join Dad outside. "So what kinds of things are we going to do to earn our Outdoor Adventure badge?" I grab a handful of stakes, ready to hand one to him.

"Let's see - hiking, fishing, orienteering . . ." Dad pauses while he hammers a stake into the ground.

I give him another one as we move to the next spot. "Orien- what?"

"Orienteering. It's a kind of mapping exercise to teach you directions."

I wrinkle my nose. "That sounds boring."

Dad grins. "Not the way Mr. Tang and I have it planned. Just wait and see." He stands up, cracks his knuckles, and gazes up at the sky. "That should do it. Just in time, too. The sun is starting to set, and I'm starving! Let's help your mom get dinner ready. Cooking is part of the badge requirements, too."

"But that's a girl's job!" I protest.

Dad laughs. "Don't let your mom hear you say that. Or all the male chefs on those cooking shows Lily watches."

I glance over at the tent and see the outline of Mortimer's antlers poking out from the top. "Uh, Dad? How are we going to get Mortimer out of the tent?"

* * *

It's a group effort, for sure. All the other families come to the rescue. The

7

stakes are removed, Mortimer guided out, and the center pole secured while the stakes are replaced. Of course, Kevin and Bradley think it's hysterical and spend more time taking pictures than actually helping.

Yes, Kevin and Bradley are also members of the Trailblazers. They've been my two least favorite people ever since my first day at Dunstan Elementary when I threw a basketball at Kevin's nose because he called me a name. I didn't mean to hurt him, but he and Bradley have held it against me ever since. Dad says the group will be good for them because it teaches self-discipline and re-sponsibility. Maybe. As long as I don't have to work with them, I'm good.

Soon all the tents are set up in a

circle and the families gather around the campfire to roast hot dogs and make s'mores. Mine is a masterpiece! I take my time and turn my stick slowly, so the marshmallow is toasted a perfect golden brown on all sides. Then I take my graham cracker and place a chocolate slice on each half. The marshmallow is placed in the center with the other half of the cracker on top. I gently squeeze together the two halves and wait patiently for the chocolate to melt.

My mouth waters in anticipation. I'm just about to take my first savory bite when Bradley hoots with laughter.

"Look at Dimmy Jimmy!" He points to me as his face drips with chocolate and gooey marshmallow. "What are you waiting for, Christmas?"

Justin springs to my defense. "Just because you already stuffed your face with three s'mores doesn't mean the rest of us have to eat like pigs."

"Alright, boys, that's enough." Dad stands up and walks around to the other side of the campfire. "Who wants to hear a scary story?"

"Me!"

"I do!"

"Yes!"

Dad begins. "A long time ago, in a forest much like this one, there was a logging camp." Dad's spooky-looking face peers over the campfire. "Late one night, two loggers heard a crash coming from an area beyond their campsite. They rushed over, only to find their metal trash can upended and the remains of their dinner gone. Deciding it was probably a bear, they went back to their campsite and settled in for the night."

I glance over at Lily, who is grabbing hold of Keiko, eyes wide.

"The next morning, they set out with buckets for a trek to the river to get water. Suddenly . . ." Dad pauses for effect. ". . . they heard the sound of breaking branches. They ducked behind a bush and watched as this huge creature munched on blackberries just several yards away. A low, growling sound came from its mouth, which slobbered with juice from the berries. Its body was covered from head to toe with shaggy dark red hair, which smelled like rotten eggs. The loggers couldn't decide if the creature was a wild animal or a human. When it stood up and bared its sharp teeth, the loggers spun around and hightailed it back to camp."

Lily lets out a shriek, which causes Bradley and Kevin to snicker. "Oh, come on, Mr. Robertson. At least make it sound realistic," Kevin says.

Dad doesn't even blink as he continues. "The next day, more loggers came into the camp. They found sleeping bags still lying by the fire and half-eaten food. But there was no sign of the two loggers. Only a trail of giant footprints - five toes spread apart and what looked like cracks and wrinkles in the ball and heel of the foot. The prints circled the campfire and headed back into the woods."

For a minute there's only silence. Then Bradley and Kevin start to laugh hysterically and point at the faces of the other kids.

"Look at them!" cries out Bradley.

"They look like they actually believe it!"

Mr. Tang says, "I remember reading about that in the paper. They called the creature Bigfoot. I believe it happened in the state of Washington, far away from here. So nothing to worry about."

"In any case," Dad says, "it's wise to follow the rules of the forest. We are only visitors, so we must respect the animals who live here. Make sure that all trash is sealed and hung up high in a tree so animals can't get to it. All food will be secured in ice chests or kept inside trailers – no food in your tent. Never go into the forest alone. You're on the buddy system while we're here. Understood?"

As everyone nods, I see Kevin lean over and mumble something to Bradley. I sure hope they aren't going to create any trouble this weekend and ruin things for everyone else.

CHAPTER 2
The Footprint

I lay in my sleeping bag, wide awake. Every howl, snort, and groan makes me think Bigfoot is out there somewhere. But then I remember Mortimer. He'll keep us safe! I learned from my animal report at school that moose don't have any enemies except Siberian tigers. And we don't have those in Wisconsin.

I must have finally drifted off to sleep, because the next thing I know, there's yelling outside the tent. I spring out of my sleeping bag and step outside into the bright morning light.

Dad and Mr. Tang are standing

next to the large pine tree where we had hung our trash last night. Both of them have their arms folded as they survey the ground. Instead of the black trash bag hanging neatly from the tree, it's been shredded and trash scattered everywhere.

Justin and I run over to them. "How did this happen?" I ask. "We did just what you said to do with the trash."

Dad rubs his chin. "This has always worked when I've gone camping before. So either some animals that can climb trees got into it, or . . ." He frowns and looks over at Mr. Tang.

"Or there's an animal that's big enough to reach the branch," finishes Mr. Tang.

"It's Bigfoot!" yells Kevin.

Bradley starts laughing so hard the dinosaur on his pajama top looks like it's dancing. "He really does exist!"

Dad inspects the ground around the trash. "Looks like there's a variety of animal tracks here, so whatever did this had lots of company." He raises his head. "You kids all get dressed and help out with breakfast while the dads get all this cleaned up. Ranger Bob will be meeting us at the campfire in an hour to talk about the hike we're taking today."

After changing into our hiking gear, we gather around the campfire and munch on eggs, bacon, and toast. I'd forgotten how much better food tastes when it's cooked over a campfire. Grandpa used to make the best skillet biscuits.

Terrance and Brian join us and

start talking about the hike.

"Man, you should have seen the hike Kevin and I took last year at Dells Pond," boasts Bradley. "It was at least five miles long and uphill – both ways!"

"Uphill both ways?" I glance at Terrance. "How is that even possible?"

"It was only a mile, and flat as this piece of toast." Terrance holds up his half-eaten toast smeared with grape jelly. "Bradley barely made it. He huffed and puffed the whole way."

Mr. Tang claps his hands. "Okay, Trailblazers, let's recite our pledge."

We all jump to our feet, remove our green Trailblazer caps, and hold up our right hands.

"A Trailblazer is smart and strives to be kind.

A Trailblazer will never leave some-one behind.

A Trailblazer is honest and friendly to all.

We pledge, on our honor, to always stand tall."

We replace our caps and sit down as a big man in a ranger uniform walks toward the center of the fire circle.

"Welcome, Trailblazers. I'm Rang-er Bob, and I'm excited to help you with your Outdoor Adventure badge this weekend. Your leaders will be giving you directions on your first task, but before that, I want to go over the rules of the forest with you."

I'm trying to figure out how tall this guy is, when I hear some giggling com-ing from behind me. I glance back to see

Kevin and Bradley tickling the back of Chelsey's neck with a stick. Every time she reaches back to scratch whatever is tickling her, they pull the stick back and try to keep from laughing out loud. Oh, brother – those two are something else. I decide to focus on Ranger Bob instead.

"You'll be going on a scavenger hunt today," Ranger Bob continues. "But it's very important for you to leave the forest exactly as you found it. So instead of picking up the items on your list, you will be taking pictures of them." He hands out small digital cameras.

Dad continues. "Except for trash, of course. The group that camped here before us didn't leave it very clean." Mr. Tang hands out black trash bags.

"What?" Kevin snorts in disgust. "I

didn't come here to be a garbage man, especially for someone else's trash. When can we go fishing?"

"Part of being a Trailblazer is working as a team," Dad says, as he passes out the list of items to find on the scavenger hunt. "I was going to let you pick your own partners, but I can choose yours for you, Kevin, if you'd rather."

My eyes grow wide. Please don't, Dad, I pray silently.

"Uh, no, that's okay, Mr. Robertson." Kevin tips his cap. "Bradley and I will be fine. We're happy to pick up any trash we happen to see." He turns to Bradley and mumbles, "We just won't see any."

Bradley covers his mouth to keep from snorting.

Dad finishes the instructions. "You must complete your list by noon, when the sun is directly overhead. So use your time wisely."

Soon we're paired up and ready to go. Mortimer clomps along behind Justin and me as we venture into the woods to find the things on the list. A pine cone, check. Smooth rock, check. Tree stump and feather, check and check. We take turns snapping pictures of each item.

I'm getting a photo of Mortimer's footprints to add to the other animal tracks we've found, when Justin calls out.

"Jimmy, come over here, quick!"

I rush over to see what Justin sounds so panicked about. His hand is shaking so badly I can hardly tell what he's pointing at.

There, in the soft soil, is this humongous footprint. It has five toes spread apart, and what looks like cracks and wrinkles in the ball and heel of the foot.

CHAPTER 3
The Investigation Begins

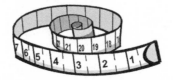

Justin pulls out a tape measure from his backpack and measures the footprint from toe to heel. "Eighteen inches long, and . . ." He stretches the tape measure across the ball of the foot. ". . . nine inches wide."

I gasp. "I've never seen a foot that big before. What do you think it could be?" I take about six photos of it.

"No human has feet that big." Justin writes down his measurements in his journal. "Let's see if there are more and where they lead."

I grab onto his jacket to stop him.

"I don't know." I put the camera in my pocket and zip it shut. "Maybe we should just go back to camp and show Dad the pictures."

"He would only ask us where we found the footprint and if there were others." Justin starts to walk in the same direction the foot is pointing. "Come on – Mortimer will protect us."

Mortimer doesn't look so sure either, but we follow Justin down the path. There are more footprints, spaced evenly apart, as if beckoning us to find the owner.

We plod deeper into the forest, until finally we reach the lake. The footsteps disappear.

"Did he walk into the lake?" Justin pulls out a pair of binoculars and peers across the water. "I don't see anything."

At this point, Mortimer nudges me in the back. I pat him on the nose. "I know, Mortimer. I think we should go back, too. Come on, Justin. Let's go and tell everyone what we found."

We hurry back to camp. Everyone is already there with their items checked off.

"Me and Kevin found two of everything!" Bradley boasts.

Kevin gives Bradley a fist bump. "Yeah. Shouldn't we get a prize or something?"

Dad sighs. "It's not a competition. Your prize will be completing your Outdoor Adventure badge. Jimmy and Justin, how did you do?"

"We found everything on the list

– and this." I take the camera out of my jacket pocket and hand it to Mr. Tang. "What do you think it is?"

Mr. Tang lets out a slow whistle as he studies the pictures. "This is unlike anything I've ever seen. What do you think?" He passes the camera to Dad. The rest of the kids gather around.

"What is it?" asks Chelsey.

"Let me see!" says Terrance.

"Well, Trailblazers, it looks like we have our own Bigfoot mystery to solve." Dad turns to Ranger Bob. "You're the wildlife expert. What do you make of this?"

Ranger Bob studies each photo. "It appears the scavenger hunt isn't over yet." Everyone cheers. "But there are some definite instructions you will need to follow. We want everyone to be safe. Some parents will need to join the hunt while others stay at the camp and keep a lookout."

"What are we searching for?" asks Brian.

Ranger Bob rattles off a list of items. "Look for any teeth, hair or fur stuck in branches or bushes, half-eaten food or trash, and any more footprints. Since this has now become an investigation, it's okay to take these items as evidence, as well as lots of pictures. I have sealable bags in this saddlebag for the evidence you find."

"Man, you're just trying to trick us into picking up trash," complains Kevin.

"Yeah, I'd much rather go fishing," whines Bradley.

Dad ignores them and continues. "Since Jimmy and Justin made the discovery, they'll lead this expedition." He turns toward Kevin and Bradley. "Solving this mystery will be much more fun than any fish you might catch, I promise."

Mr. Tang adds, "And remember, Trailblazers. You're working as a team here. Help each other and share what you find. Report back to camp in an hour and we'll compare discoveries."

Ranger Bob hoists me onto Mortimer's hump and tosses the saddlebag across his back. Justin and I lead the group to the spot where we found the first footprint. Chelsey and Brittany take off into the bushes to look for any signs of food or more footprints. Brian peers up into the trees. Kevin and Bradley just stand off to the side making fun of everyone. I pretend they aren't even there and slide off Mortimer's back to get a closer look.

Terrance surveys the area around the footprint with a magnifying glass, like some kind of detective. "Hey, Jimmy, I think I found something! Bring me a plastic bag, will ya?"

I run to grab some packets from the saddlebag on Mortimer's back. "What is it?" I open the bag for Terrance to deposit his find – two yellow teeth the size of quarters.

"Wow, look what I found!" cries out Justin. He holds up a half-eaten piece of hot dog, probably from our trash last night.

"Ew, gross!" says Allison. "I found

some more footprints over here in some dried mud. I'm taking pictures of them so I don't have to get my hands all yucky."

Dad claps his hands to get everybody's attention. "Great job, Trailblazers. Now gather around. Let's compare what everyone found before we head back to camp to examine all of it."

As the discoveries are shared, Justin whispers to me. "Where's Kevin and Bradley?"

I glance back to where I last saw them. No one there. "I don't know. They probably went back to camp to get out of having to do any work."

"I hope so," Justin says. "I sure wouldn't want to be out here in the forest if there really is a big creature hiding somewhere."

There's a gasp from the group as everyone holds their noses when Chelsey and Brittany show what they found.

Chelsey holds up a clear plastic bag revealing the scariest find yet – a clump of dark red hair that smells like rotten eggs, stuck to a branch with blackberries.

CHAPTER 4
Super Sleuths

We hurry back to camp and find tables equipped with different kinds of scientific equipment. Microscopes, magnifying glasses, pictures of different animal tracks, small hammers and chisels, and a variety of brushes cover the picnic tables. Ranger Bob assigns us to groups as he hands out journals and pencils.

He points to the table with Brittany, Chelsey, and Terrance. "You are in charge of sifting through the teeth and hair you found. Clean them carefully and then look at each piece under a microscope. Record what you observe."

Brian and Allison are assigned the task of going through the food that was found, although Allison protests, "This stuff is gross! Do I have to touch it?"

Ranger Bob hands each of them plastic gloves to wear. "Use the magnifying glasses to see if you can find any teeth marks and draw pictures of them in your journals."

Dad looks around and frowns. "Has anyone seen Kevin and Bradley?

Bradley's dad looks up from his camping chair, where he apparently had spent the afternoon on his iPad while the rest of us were looking for clues. "They probably went to the fishing hole. I'll find them." He grunts as he rises out of the chair and takes one last sip of lemonade.

"Be careful, dear," calls out Mrs.

Spencer, as he trudges across the camp-ground.

Justin and I get back to our examination of the footprint photos and compare them to the pictures of different animal tracks to see if we can find any that look similar. Mortimer peers over my shoulder and snorts.

"Yes, I know, Mortimer," I say. "The footprints were obviously not made by you or any of your forest friends." Mortimer looks bored and trots off to go play with Lily and Keiko.

Justin squints as he focuses on one of the photos. "Plus, the pattern of these footprints doesn't look like they're made by a four-legged creature." He wrinkles his forehead. "But what animal walks on two legs?"

"Maybe a gorilla?" I suggest.

"A gorilla wouldn't be in the forest." Justin studies the animal tracks closer. "And there's no zoo nearby where one could have escaped. Besides, they only walk on two legs some of the time. These pictures show something walking totally on two legs the whole time."

Lucky for us Justin wants to be a zoologist when he grows up. He sure knows a lot about wild animals.

There is silence for a moment, and I can hear Lily and Keiko chanting a rhyme while they play jump rope:

"Teddy bear, Teddy bear, turn around,

Teddy bear, Teddy bear, touch the ground."

I glance over to the campfire area,

and just like my first day at Dunstan Elementary, there's Mortimer, turning one end of the jump rope while Keiko turns the other. Lily jumps in the center and continues chanting:

"Teddy bear, Teddy bear, touch your shoe,

Teddy bear, Teddy bear, that will do."

A thought hits me and I turn back to Justin. "What about a bear? You did your school report on that. I remember you saying that bears walk on two legs a lot."

Justin holds his chin in one hand and strokes it like a beard. He has a funny habit of doing that while he's concentrating. He thinks it makes him look more intelligent.

"That's true, they do." He points to the animal tracks. "But compare the footprints. Bears have long, sharp claws that curve at the end. That would definitely show up in a footprint. Our creature has what can only be described as toes . . . human-like toes."

Ranger Bob stands over us and listens to our discussion. "You boys are on the right track. Keep digging for answers."

"But Ranger Bob, what is it? It can't possibly be human, can it?" I start to look up when I notice Ranger Bob's feet – the biggest ones I've ever seen!

"You're getting there. Don't give up." Ranger Bob turns to the rest of the group. "All right, gather around and tell us what you found."

As the rest of the kids circle Ranger Bob, I whisper to Justin. "Look at his huge feet! What do you think? Is he playing some sort of a joke on us?"

Justin stares at Ranger Bob's boots. "Naw, I doubt it. There's gotta be some kind of code among park rangers not to play tricks on little kids. Let's go see what the others figured out."

We both stand up and start walking toward the group. "I still think . . ."

I don't have a chance to finish my sentence. It's interrupted by a horrific scream coming from the forest.

CHAPTER 5
Bigfoot Juice

Mortimer drops the jump rope and gallops into the forest, heading in the direction of the scream. I've never seen him move that fast! Ranger Bob follows, as Dad and Mr. Tang try to keep the rest of us in the camp.

"What's going on?" Lily and Keiko run over to us. They grab on to Mom and Mrs. Tang for support. We hear more screams for help echoing through the trees.

I turn to Justin. "Could it be Kevin and Bradley?"

As much as I dislike them, I sure hope they didn't run into Bigfoot. What else could it be? Even if it's not Bigfoot, could they have disturbed a bear? Maybe a skunk sprayed them! A zillion thoughts float through my mind – none of them good.

No one seems to move as time ticks away. The silence is finally broken when Mortimer crashes through the trees. Bradley's dad, Mr. Spencer, is on Mortimer's back, hanging on to his antlers. Kevin and Bradley walk ahead, heads down and dragging their feet, as Mortimer pushes them with his huge snout to keep them moving. Ranger Bob brings up the rear of this little parade, carrying a net and shaking his head.

"What happened?" "Are you okay?" "Did you catch Bigfoot?" The group rushes toward Mortimer with questions for Ranger Bob as he helps Mr. Spencer down.

Bradley glares and points at me. "It's all his fault . . ." My mouth drops open as I stare back in disbelief.

Mr. Spencer interrupts, his face red with anger. "Son, be quiet and go sit down. You, too, Kevin." He points toward a log by the campfire circle.

The Trailblazers and their families circle around Bradley's dad to hear his explanation. Ranger Bob grabs a couple of stumps so Mr. Spencer can sit down and prop up his leg.

"This is my fault," he begins. "While all of you were out searching for evidence of this Bigfoot creature, I went online to do some research. I found a website about people who have actually conducted searches and discovered the same things you guys did. One person had used this concoction called Bigfoot Juice. So when Bradley and Kevin came back early, I had them find all the ingredients so we could make some – berries, raw eggs, olive oil, and herbs."

"Nasty smelling stuff," Bradley says, but immediately zips his mouth shut when his dad glares at him.

"I continued to investigate how the Bigfoot Juice was used, and I guess I lost track of the time," Mr. Spencer goes on. "When I went to find the boys, they had disappeared. Apparently, they found the cargo net I keep in my truck, and decided to set out on their own to catch Bigfoot."

Justin leans over to me and whispers, "And we thought they didn't believe in Bigfoot."

Now it's my turn to snort.

Bradley's dad takes a deep breath as he grimaces in pain. He reaches over to rub his ankle as he goes on. "I followed their footprints into the forest. I thought about calling out their names, but decided they needed to be taught a good lesson. So I hiked silently through the trees, focusing on their footprints on the ground. What I didn't see was the net that was strung up between two trees. I hafta say, they did a great job of covering it up with leaves and pine needles. The next thing I knew, I was hanging upside down in the air, the boys below me screaming their heads off!"

Ranger Bob continues the story. "When Mortimer and I arrived, I managed to lower the net enough to get Mr. Spencer onto Mortimer's back. Then I cut the net and untangled it. It was partially wrapped around his ankle, however, which I'm afraid might be broken. But we won't know until I get Mr. and Mrs. Spencer to the hospital for an X-ray."

At this point, Bradley's mom rushes toward her husband and throws her arms around his neck. "Oh, my poor, sweet Honey Bear. Are you in much pain?" She turns to Dad and Mr. Tang. "Shame on you two for initiating such a dangerous activity. Someone could have died!" She clicks her tongue as she helps Mr. Spencer to Ranger Bob's jeep.

Bradley runs over to his parents. "I wanna go with you, Mummy and Daddy!"

Mrs. Spencer stops to hug Bradley. "Oh no, Bradleykins, you stay here with Kevin and his parents." She heaves a huge sigh and wipes a tear from her eye. "We'll be fine." She tosses her hair back and climbs into the jeep beside her husband. Ranger Bob jumps into the driver's seat and soon they roar down the dirt road toward the highway.

I look over at Bradley, who is staring at the jeep as it leaves. His shoulders quiver and tears leave brown streaks down his dirty cheeks.

I lean toward Justin and say, "Bradleykins?"

"Yeah, not much drama in that family, is there?" Justin grins. "Seriously, no one was going to die, especially from a twisted ankle."

Dad and Mr. Tang stand by the campfire in a deep discussion. Finally, they face the group and Dad clears his throat.

"I'm sure Bud Spencer will be fine," he says. "From my experience as a fire-fighter, I've seen many injuries like his, and the ankle doesn't appear to be broken. But it's best to be cautious, so an X-ray at the hospital will tell more."

Chelsey steps forward. "But what about Bigfoot? What happens to all our evidence?"

Mr. Tang smiles, but shakes his head. "Yeah, about that. Mr. Robertson and I have a confession to make." He looks over at Dad, who nods. "The purpose of the weekend was to teach you the basics in outdoor survival to earn your Outdoor Adventure badge. A big part of that is learning how to work as a team."

"And rather than do the usual orienteering and other team building activities, we decided to let you all have some fun with the project." Dad reaches into a large gunny sack and pulls out two short poles with rubberized feet attached.

A loud gasp erupts from the group. My eyes widen as I realize Dad had made those footprints, not Bigfoot.

"You lied to us?" Kevin shouts. "I was right – you tricked us into picking up trash and wouldn't let us go fishing. And now Bradley's dad is hurt because of you!"

Other parents look at each other and murmur, shaking their heads.

Mr. Tang holds up his hands and tries to calm everyone down. "In all fairness, Mr. Robertson and I were trying to be creative. We didn't lie to you – we created evidence just as it's been reported in other searches, and we let you draw your own conclusions. You did a great job of finding the evidence, asking questions, and problem solving."

Dad's stern face focuses on Kevin and Bradley. "Mr. Spencer only got hurt because you boys didn't follow directions and went off on your own. If you had stayed with the group, that wouldn't have happened."

Kevin narrows his eyes but doesn't say anything. Bradley just pushes dirt around with his shoe and doesn't look up.

Mr. Tang puts his hand on Dad's shoulder. "Regardless of how this happened, as leaders of the Trailblazers, we take responsibility for things getting out of hand. One of us should have made sure everyone was following directions. That's part of growing up – admitting when something goes wrong and owning up to it."

"So, let's all call it quits for the day and put today's activity behind us," Dad says. "We still have tomorrow to enjoy fishing and hiking."

I don't move. I can't believe what I'm hearing. In my whole life, my dad has always been honest with me.

Kevin and Bradley pass by me on the way to their tent. Bradley's eyes are now dry of tears. He gives me the dirtiest look ever but doesn't say anything. Kevin, of course, can't keep his mouth shut.

"You'll be sorry, Dimmy Jimmy,"

he sneers. "You and your dad will wish you never moved here."

My first impulse is to deck Kevin, but my arm won't move. Instead, I turn and bolt away from him, past my mom and dad, and into the tent. I climb into my sleeping bag, shoes and all, and zip it shut. I'm never speaking to anyone, ever again.

CHAPTER 6
Operation Footprint

I fight to hold back the tears, when I hear something rustling at the entrance of the tent. I turn over and find myself staring into Mortimer's Oreo-sized eyes, his head and antlers poked inside. He licks my face like he's trying to tell me everything will be okay.

"No, Mortimer, things are not going to be okay. I wish Grandpa was here to tell me what to do." Whenever I found myself in a bad situation, Grandpa used to say, "If it is to be, it's up to me." But I don't see how that's going to help me now.

I hear Mom and Dad talking outside the tent. They keep their voices lowered, so I can barely make out what they say.

"I didn't lie to him, Catherine," Dad says.

"Well, you weren't exactly honest with him, either."

I peek under the tent and see Mom standing with her arms folded, the way she looks when I'm the one in trouble.

"It was supposed to be fun." Dad starts pacing back and forth. "And I think they were having fun, until Kevin and Bradley decided to go off on their own. What was Bud Spencer thinking, leading them on a wild goose chase with that Bigfoot Juice concoction?"

"I think he's suffering the conse-quences of his actions," Mom says. "Now you need to go in there and talk to your son."

I duck back into my sleeping bag and pretend to be asleep. Mortimer gives me a final lick and pulls his head back outside. Soon the zipper of the tent opens all the way and Dad crawls in. He sits by my sleeping bag for a minute or two before speaking.

"I know you're not asleep, Jimmy," he says gently. "I can see your eyelids flickering."

That's what happens when you have a dad that's a firefighter with first-aid training. I slowly turn over to face him, but I'm still not going to say anything.

"You're upset, and I don't blame

you," Dad begins. "Mr. Tang and I thought making fake footprints to resemble Bigfoot's would be a big adventure for the group, and a great way to work as a team. We never expected it to backfire like that."

I sit up and break my vow not to talk. "Everything backfires when Kevin and Bradley are involved. And now they're saying it's all my fault and we'll be sorry we ever moved here. I already am."

I try to blink away the tears, but I'm not very successful and they slide down my cheeks. I sniff and wipe my eyes with my sleeve.

Dad hands me a tissue. "Well, I'm not sorry we moved here. We're reliving all the memories of summers with Grandpa, and his friend Charlie next door, and all their funny stories of growing up together. You've made good friends with Justin, Terrance, Chelsey, and the others." He stops and chuckles as Mortimer pokes his head in again. "And of course, Mortimer. You would have never met him if we'd stayed in Arizona."

I blow my nose while Mortimer bugles in reply. Dad and I both laugh and he gives me a big hug.

"I'm sorry I let you down, son," he says.

"But what about Kevin and Bradley?" I ask.

"Well, it seems that Mr. Spencer is none too happy with them either." Dad glances at his watch. "Ranger Bob brought the Spencers back from the hospital a few minutes ago. Bud's ankle isn't broken, but it's a bad sprain. So he has a big boot on his foot and has to use crutches for a couple of weeks. He says he has a plan to teach those two a lesson they'll never forget."

Now I'm interested. "What is it?"

"I can't tell you right now. We still need to work out the details." Dad starts toward the tent entrance. "But we'll need your help – Mortimer's, too. Get some shut-eye, and as soon as everyone in camp is asleep, Mr. Spencer and I will go into the forest to put 'Operation Footprint' into place. You and Mortimer will do your part in the morning. Lily is staying with Keiko tonight, and Mom and I will be in later." He steps around Mortimer's antlers and goes outside, leaving me alone with Mortimer.

"What do you think, Mortimer?"

He snorts and shakes his head.

"Yeah, I'm not sure either. What if this plan backfires, too?"

There's no way I'm going to get any sleep. Instead, I stare at the bouncing shadows on the tent wall and hope I'm not going to regret this.

CHAPTER 7
More Footprints

I must have fallen asleep, since it's daylight when I wake up to screams. Again. My heart pounds as I pull on my jeans as fast as I can and scoot outside.

Instead of Bigfoot or any other huge animal, I see Kevin and Bradley, still in their pajamas, running across the meadow like they're in the 50-yard dash. Chasing them are two raccoons, candy wrappers hanging out of their mouths. Concerned faces on the adults turn into laughter, as the boys run around in circles until the raccoons finally bound off into the forest.

Kevin and Bradley return to the campground, gasping for air as their shoulders heave up and down. Dad and Mr. Tang meet them at the campfire circle and wait for them to sit down and catch their breath.

"What did we tell you about keeping food in your tent?" demands Mr. Tang, holding up a candy wrapper one of the raccoons dropped.

"Not to do it," mutters Bradley. He sits on a log and draws in the dirt with a stick.

Kevin squints up at our troop leaders. "But we kept the candy in a Tupperware container hidden in our sleeping bags. We didn't think any animal would find it there."

Dad tries to keep from smiling. "Haven't you seen those YouTube videos of raccoons and how nimble their paws are? They're like little human hands. Why, I've even seen a raccoon unscrew the lid of a jar of peanut butter."

Mr. Tang folds his arms. "Look, Trailblazers, our rules were created for a reason. We didn't make them up to prevent you from having fun."

"The rules were designed to keep you safe," adds Dad. "You were lucky those were harmless raccoons and not a bear that found your candy."

Bradley looks up and sighs. "We're sorry."

"Well, sorry or not, there are consequences for this stunt," says Mr. Tang.

"You two will pick up trash around the campground while the rest of us go on our hike to the fishing hole."

Kevin starts to protest, but snaps his mouth shut instead.

* * *

The campers are sitting at the tables enjoying breakfast when Chelsey comes running up.

"Hey, you guys, I was just coming out of the bathroom and you'll never believe what I found!"

Groans of "Not again," and "What now?" echo through the campground. My eyes widen and I glance at Dad.

He winks at me and says, "Well, then, I guess we better go take a look!"

Chelsey leads the Trailblazers to the comfort station surrounded by trees on the other side of the campfire circle. She points to the soft ground that leads to the door, and sure enough, there's a huge footprint. But there's only one, not two. And on either side of it are two small round circles.

Mr. Tang bends down to take a closer look. "Well, Trailblazers, what do you think?"

Kevin pipes up. "I think this is another lie and I want nothing to do with it." He turns to Bradley. "Come on, let's go get the dumb trash picked up so we can have some fun later."

Mr. Spencer yells after them as they leave. "Stay within eyesight of the campground, boys, do you hear me? Do not go into the forest!"

Kevin waves his hand in the air

without looking back. Mr. Spencer shakes his head and turns back to the group. We ignore Kevin and Bradley and study the strange footprints instead.

Brian clears his throat. "I don't think it looks like an animal or a human, because there are no toes or claws."

"And there's only one footprint, not two," adds Brittany. "What has only one foot?"

"A flamingo?" suggests Lily.

I groan. "There aren't any flamingos in a forest, silly."

"I once had a parrot that could stand on one foot," says Terrance. "And other wading birds do that, too."

Allison squats down to take a picture. "But none of those would make a huge footprint like this one."

Justin strokes his chin. "It looks more like a boot than a footprint. But what about the two round circles? What would make those?"

We take out the papers from the day before of all the different animal prints. I think the rabbit's looks the closest, but why would a boot print be between two rabbit prints?

"Maybe it's Mortimer," says Brian. But one look at Mortimer's footprints clearly shows that it's not him.

Silence surrounds us until I get an idea. "I know what it is!" I shout.

All heads turn to stare at me. I inhale and hold my breath for a moment, letting it out slowly. It's a technique Grandpa taught me to help calm down.

"It's him!" I point to Mr. Spencer, standing at the edge of the group on crutches. A huge boot protects his sprained ankle.

Mr. Spencer's face turns red as an apple. "When ya gotta go, ya gotta go."

Another thought comes to me. "But what about your good foot? Where's its footprint?"

Mr. Spencer flattens his lips and looks down at his feet – one in the protective boot and the other one bare. "I was too lazy to put on my other shoe, and I didn't want my bare foot to get dirty, so I just left it up in the air as I walked with the crutches. You know, you're pretty smart to figure that out, Jimmy."

Dad grins and gives a thumbs up.

Justin high-fives me. "Way to go, Sherlock!"

The rest of the Trailblazers start to cheer and pound me on the back, and Mortimer practically licks my face off.

Just when I think I've solved the mystery of all mysteries, Kevin and Bradley rush in to break up the celebration.

Trash bags in hand, they both start talking at the same time and so fast that no one can understand them.

"Boys, slow down!" yells Mr. Tang. "Now, one at a time – what's wrong?

Sweat pours down Bradley's face as he breathes heavily. "We saw . . . they're huge . . . and weird looking . . . and . . ."

Dad pinches his eyebrows together and turns to Kevin. "What did you see?"

Kevin gulps. "Footprints . . . we saw footprints."

Everyone groans.

"Are you kidding me?"

"Now who's making stuff up?"

"Why should we believe you?"

Mr. Tang turns to Dad, looking puzzled. "Did you plan another team building exercise?"

Dad shakes his head. "No, did you?"

Mr. Tang's eyes get real big. "No, I didn't."

CHAPTER 8
He Who Laughs Last . . .

It doesn't take us long to follow Kevin and Bradley out to the area where they were picking up trash. Sure enough, there are these strange web-shaped footprints about the size of the Bigfoot ones.

Kevin bends over the prints, hands on his knees. "At first I thought it was another trick by our scout leaders, since everyone was going to the lake today. But that didn't make any sense, because the fishing hole is way over at the other end of the lake. So nobody would have come this way."

"And no one knew we would be picking up trash here," adds Bradley.

"What do you think it is, Mr. Robertson?" asks Allison.

Dad squats down by the prints to take a closer look. Finally he shrugs. "I have no idea." He turns to Mr. Tang, who just shakes his head.

"It looks like a giant duck," suggests Bradley.

Justin says, "It would have to be a six-foot duck to make footprints that big!" Everyone laughs and we start to make our own ridiculous suggestions.

"It's Big Bird!" snorts Brian.

"Or Barney the Dinosaur," adds Chelsey, giggling.

Brittany stands with her hands on her hips. "I think you all have been watching too much Dino Train on TV."

"Be quiet!" shouts Kevin. "This is serious, you guys. Something made these prints and it's still lurking out there somewhere."

"Yeah, just waiting to attack one of us," Bradley chimes in.

Everyone shushes while Kevin continues. "Here's my theory – a duck-billed platypus!"

Mr. Tang was silent for a moment. "Well, that would be a good guess . . ."

Kevin stands up and puffs out his chest, glaring at all the Trailblazers.

". . . if we were in Australia," Mr. Tang finishes.

"Ha Ha, Kevin." Terrance starts to taunt Kevin and Bradley until he gets the "look" from Dad. "Sorry," he mumbles.

"What about a Spinosaurus?" asks Bradley. "I saw in a book that their footprints look just like this!" His face actually looks serious.

Nobody laughs. I look over at Justin and raise my eyebrows.

Justin leans over and whispers, "Bradley has been obsessed with dinosaurs since pre-school and still thinks they're alive."

Kevin stands with his arms folded while tapping one foot. He's obviously angry that they're not being taken seriously. "You all believed Jimmy's dad when he told a story about Bigfoot. And that wasn't even true!"

Bradley stands beside Kevin, hands in his pockets, and glares at the group. "Yeah, and my dad risked his life to prove it was all a hoax."

"And now, right in front of you, are footprints no one can explain," continues Kevin. "And you laugh at us!"

"Like you laughed at us when we were gathering Bigfoot evidence?" sneers Justin.

Then it's like a volcano erupted, with everyone yelling and taunting and blaming all at once. Dad and Mr. Tang clap their hands to try and calm everyone down, but the noise gets so loud I have to cover my ears or I'm afraid my head will explode.

Then this deafening bugle blast pierces through the noise and echoes beyond the forest. Everyone turns to see where it came from and what made such a horrible sound.

There, parked beside a tree, wearing swimming fins on his front feet and goggles over his eyes, stands Mortimer.

CHAPTER 9
Gone Fishing

There's silence for a moment, and then Chelsey and Allison start giggling. Soon everyone joins in. Mortimer adds a couple of bugle calls.

Dad strolls over to Mortimer and takes off the goggles. "Well, Mortimer, you certainly look like something out of a science fiction movie."

"Yeah, we can call him 'Aqua-Moose'!" Bradley grabs his stomach as it jiggles from him laughing so hard.

"Or 'Mortimer the Swamp Thing'," giggles Brittany.

Kevin just stands there with his arms folded, his mouth pressed into a straight line. He's obviously not amused by any of this. "How about 'Mortimer the big, fat liar'?"

I bend down to take the flippers off Mortimer's front hoofs. "Mortimer hasn't done anything wrong. If you want to blame somebody, blame me."

A hush falls over the group as everyone stares at me.

My face is so warm I feel like my freckles are about to pop off. "I did this. I'm the one who put the swimming fins on Mortimer to make the footprints."

Terrance frowns. "But why, Jimmy? Were you trying to trick us, too?"

I shake my head. "I wasn't trying to trick anybody. I guess I wanted to show Kevin and Bradley how it feels to be laughed at." I turn to face my mortal enemies. "It doesn't feel very good, does it?"

Dad steps forward, Mr. Spencer close behind him. "Jimmy is not totally responsible for this," Dad says. "It was Mr. Spencer's idea to plant his footprints at the comfort station in the middle of the night. Jimmy and I brought Mortimer here before breakfast to make the web footprints. I figured Kevin and Bradley would choose to pick up trash here, because it's close to the lake."

Bradley gasps. "Dad? You were in on this, too? How could you?"

Mr. Spencer put his arm around Bradley's shoulders. "It's time you and Kevin stop picking on other kids and learn to get along with them instead. I was hoping being a member of the Trailblazers would help you see how important it is to be part of a group."

Bradley kicks at one of the footprints. "I really was hoping it was a Spinosaurus."

Kevin snorts. "You know they're extinct, don't you?"

"Of course I do!" retorts Bradley. "It's just fun pretending they're real sometimes."

"Like Bigfoot?" I say, looking at Dad.

He winks at me and says, "So what do you say we all go fishing?"

"Yay!" shout the Trailblazers.

Bradley and Kevin shrug and pick up their trash bags to get back to work.

I nod to Justin and he gestures to Brian and Terrance. We all grab trash bags and join in.

Kevin stops and scowls. "What are you guys doing?"

I just keep working. "We're a team, remember?"

Suddenly I have an idea. I hang my trash bag from Mortimer's antlers and slam dunk a handful of garbage. "Two points!"

Soon we're all dunking trash in the bag while Mortimer lets out a bugle call every time we score. We start laughing so hard I get the hiccups, which makes everyone howl even more.

It doesn't take long for the area to look like someone had used a vacuum cleaner.

"Come on!" shouts Kevin. "Let's catch up with the rest of the group."

* * *

Later, we're sitting at the fishing hole, waiting for tugs on our lines. Dad used to take me fishing at the lake in Arizona. When I was little, I would keep asking how much longer before a fish would nibble on my bait. His answer was always, "You need to be patient, Jimmy." Not my strong point.

"I got something! I got something!" Allison screeches.

Mr. Tang rushes over to help her reel it in. You would have thought it was the size of a whale, the way she struggles and grunts to bring it in. When it finally breaks the surface, her line is covered with long strands of wet grass. And at the end of the line – a teeny, tiny fish.

Kevin cracks up. "It looks like a sardine! Allison caught a sardine!"

Allison wrinkles her nose. "Oooh, it smells fishy." She reaches out and touches it. "And it's slimy – yuck!"

Mr. Tang chuckles. "Good job, Allison, but that won't even make an appetizer for one person, let alone supper for all of us. Let me throw it back for you."

The rest of us turn our attention back to our own lines, watching the water in anticipation. The wind blows gently through the trees and creates ripples in the water. It's so hypnotizing I almost fall asleep.

Then a loud splash breaks the silence. My eyes pop open and focus on what's making the noise.

There, in the middle of the fishing hole is Mortimer. He lowers his huge head into the water and comes back up with his antlers full of fish. He wades to the shore and plops the fish down next to me. Then he plods back out and returns with another bunch of fish. He drops them next to Kevin, whose eyes bug out like a cartoon character.

Mortimer continues to go back and forth until every Trailblazer has several fish piled next to them. There's plenty for all of us, including our families. We bag everything up and hang the sacks full of fish onto Mortimer's back. Then we trudge back to camp, competing in a whistling contest to see who has the loudest whistle or can blow a tune that everyone recognizes. I think this is the most fun I've had since the teachers versus the third grade soccer game.

Back at the campground we feast on the mouth-watering fish that Mortimer caught for us. Except for Bradley, who scarfs down three hot dogs instead.

"I only like to catch 'em, not eat 'em," he mumbles between bites.

After dinner, we gather around

the campfire for our Outdoor Adventure badge ceremony. Ranger Bob assists Dad and Mr. Tang in handing out the badges to each Trailblazer.

"This has been a very interesting weekend, Trailblazers," Dad begins. "Mr. Tang and I had a goal to create an experience that would teach you how to work together. Although things did not go exactly as planned . . ." He gestures over to Mr. Spencer, who holds up a crutch. ". . . I think you'll all agree that we learned a lot about human nature, forgiveness . . ."

". . . and footprints!" adds Bradley.

Dad chuckles. "And footprints."

Mr. Tang continues, "I know you've all heard the expression that there is no 'I' in the word 'Team.' It all comes down to listening to each other and respecting one another. Something that will be a part of you for the rest of your lives."

"We are proud of each and every one of you," adds Dad. "And we hope you've all grown up just a little bit this weekend." He pauses to look at each Trailblazer individually, but his eyes rest just a little longer on Kevin and Bradley. "Well, enough of the serious talk. We have an early morning tomorrow to break camp and head home." Everyone groans. "But first . . . who's ready for scary stories around the campfire?"

"NO!!!" Everyone shouts in unison. "No more stories!"

CHAPTER 10
It Can't Be . . . Can it?

"This summer just isn't going to be the same without Grandpa." I try to throw a rock across the lake to see how many times it bounces before it sinks. Instead, it plops right in. "He used to be able to skip his rock at least five times."

"My dad says it's all in the wrist." Justin grins and aims his flat stone. It skims across the surface three times before sinking.

I sigh and put my head down, pretending to look for the perfect rock. I feel a nudge in my back and turn around to see Mortimer with a flat stone hanging out of his mouth. His eyes seem to say, "Try it again."

I wipe the slobber off on my jeans and position my fingers around the rock like Grandpa showed me last summer. I take a deep breath as I flick my wrist back and forth three times before letting go. Straight shot to the water . . . one . . . two . . . plop!

"You're getting closer," Justin said. "What is it your Grandpa used to say?"

"If it is to be, it's up to me," I respond. "I miss him."

"Yeah, I get that." Justin picks up another rock. "My grandma died before school started last year. Chinese New Year wasn't the same without her sticky rice cakes." He tries to flick a pebble between Mortimer's antlers, but Mortimer knocks it away.

I pick up a branch and attempt to hit a rock into the lake. "Grandpa promised he'd help Dad build a treehouse for me this year. Guess it's just going to be a boring old summer instead."

"Hey boys!" Dad calls from the campground. "Come and help get things ready. It's time to head home."

I rub the Outdoor Adventure badge hanging from my neck, as if it might bring good luck. "Well, this was fun anyway."

Justin and I walk with Mortimer back to the campground. "Yeah, searching for Bigfoot was really cool, even though it turned out to be a 'team building' exercise, as my dad calls it." Justin puts "team building" in air quotes.

I grin. "Well, at least Kevin and Bradley got a taste of their own medicine, as my Grandpa would say."

Soon we're all chipping in to break camp – taking down tents, rolling up sleeping bags, bagging up food. Ranger Bob makes sure that campfires aren't smoldering or trash left behind.

With the vehicles loaded and ready to go, Ranger Bob calls us over one last time. He towers over the Trailblazers gathered around him like chickens. I glance behind him and see that with his ranger hat on, his shadow almost resembles . . . Bigfoot? I shake those thoughts from my head. I've definitely had enough of Bigfoot this weekend.

"Trailblazers, it's been an exciting

weekend, hasn't it?" Ranger Bob says. "I hope you've learned a lot about taking care of the forest and working together to accomplish a goal. I'm very glad to have been a part of it and I hope you'll come back again soon."

With a chorus of goodbyes, we climb into our cars and trucks. I give Mortimer one final hug before he heads back into the forest. I call "shotgun" and jump into the front passenger seat.

Mom stands by the open door, arms folded across her chest. "Jimmy, you know the rules. In the back seat with your sister, please."

"Aw, Mom!" My protests don't do any good. I help Lily buckle the seat belt in her booster seat, thankful I grew out of mine last year. I wave to Justin and his family as they pass by, their truck hauling their pop-up trailer. Behind them is the Spencer family, with Bradley's mom driving since Mr. Spencer can't with his big boot. Bradley makes a goofy face, as usual.

The rest of the Trailblazers and their families drive in a single file line toward the highway. When Kevin's car goes by, he just sneers at me. Some things never change, I guess. Our van is the last to leave.

Finally on the highway, we travel in silence for a while. Then Dad glances back at me in the rearview mirror. "So what was your favorite part about the weekend?"

"I liked making s'mores," pipes up Lily. "They were yummy!"

Mom laughs. "Although I wasn't fond of the sticky cleanup afterwards. The campfire was nice, though."

Dad looks at me again. "And you, Jimmy? What was your favorite part?"

I narrow my eyes and think back over the weekend. "The scavenger hunt was fun – taking pictures of what we found. And acting like CSI agents with the microscopes was cool."

"Even though Bigfoot turned out to be a hoax?" The hopeful look on Dad's face makes it seem like he's trying to apologize.

A sudden gasp from Mom causes us to peer out the front window. The vehicles in front of us are all slowing down – crimson tail lights lined up like Christmas decorations.

Dad slams on his brakes to avoid hitting Kevin's truck in front of us. "Why is everyone slowing down?" He steers the van over toward the right side of the highway.

Mom leans out the window and pushes her sunglasses up on her head. "It looks like there's some sort of animal walking across the meadow up ahead."

"Everyone must be slowing down to be sure they don't hit it," says Dad.

We cruise like a turtle for a little while. Some of the kids ahead of us stick their heads out the windows and point at something. Road construction keeps everyone from pulling off the road onto the shoulder.

"It's probably just Mortimer," I say, real casual-like. "Geez, you'd think they never saw him before."

We inch closer. Mom still has her head out the window. "It's Mortimer, all right, but there's something with him."

"What is it?" Lily bounces around in her seat trying to see.

Mom squints. "I can't quite make out what it is. It's definitely taller than Mortimer."

I lean over the front seat and hand her my binoculars. She focuses them on what's ahead, but quickly ducks back into the car and rolls up the window.

Mom stares wide-eyed at Dad. "You're not going to believe this."

"What?" I try to roll down the window, but Mom locks it before I can get it open. "Why won't you let me see?"

"Wait until we get closer," says Dad.

"Then we can all see it together."

I'm about to pee my pants, I'm so excited to see what kind of animal is with Mortimer. After all, Mortimer is friends with everyone in the forest. But something that's taller than him? A bear walking upright? Maybe it's another moose. I feel like a detective all over again.

As we get closer, I can see Kevin's head in the back seat of the truck ahead. He looks like he's tearing his hair out. He whips his head around to face us and starts pointing over toward the meadow. He's mouthing something, but I can't make out what it is.

Finally we get within sight of what everyone is so worked up about. Mom cries out, Lily squeals, and Dad grips his hands on the steering wheel. He tries to keep his eyes on the road while turning to stare at what we all can't believe.

Walking beside Mortimer, clear as day in the bright sunlight, is Bigfoot.

CHAPTER 11
Grandpa's Secret

The car seems to move in slow motion as we stare at the creature. I grab my binoculars back from Mom to get a closer look. Matted red hair covers its entire body, and twigs and burrs stick out at all angles. Drool drips from its mouth as it tramps alongside Mortimer like they're old friends. There's nothing else this creature could possibly be except Bigfoot.

Mortimer snorts and nudges Bigfoot toward the forest as the cars creep by. A moment later, Bigfoot gallops into the trees with Mortimer on his heels. The highway disappears into a tunnel. By the time we come out the other side, Mortimer and Bigfoot are nowhere to be seen.

That's when I realize I still have the camera in my pocket. "Stop the car!" I shout. "We need to go after them!"

"It's not safe," Dad replies, as he follows the other cars down the highway. "And by the time we're able to turn around and head back, they'll be long gone anyway."

I sit and pout, watching the cars ahead and wondering what the rest of the Trailblazers are thinking. I can see Kevin pounding on the seat in front of him, obviously trying to get his dad to stop also. No one else seems to be having any luck with that either.

We continue down the road in

silence. Mom turns around to check on Lily and me. She flashes a weak smile and pats my hand.

Finally Dad speaks. "I don't know what to say. I have no idea what that was. No clue, whatsoever."

"It was Bigfoot," Lily says, like that's the most logical explanation.

"Was it?" Dad glances into the rearview mirror. "Or someone dressed to look like Bigfoot? I really don't know."

Lily smiles. "Charlie would know."

I let out a snort. "Why do you think Charlie would know?" Like Grandpa's old friend who lives next door would know that Bigfoot lives in the forest near Peabody, Wisconsin.

"Because he's lived here his whole life and he knows lots of things." Lily slurps from her water bottle. "He showed me a scrapbook of lots of pictures of him and Grandpa camping when they were kids."

I shake my head in disbelief. "When do you go over to Charlie's house?"

"Some days after school I go visit him," Lily says. "He gets lonely some-times. He says he misses his checker games with Grandpa, so I like to play with him. Sometimes he even lets me win." Her toothless grin makes me smile. I never let Lily beat me at checkers.

Mom's cell phone rings as we head down the street toward our house. "Yes, Shana, we saw it. No, we have no idea what it was." She looks at Dad and rais-es her eyebrows. "I really don't think . . . okay, I'll let Matt know."

"What did Shana want?" Dad pulls the van into our driveway.

Mom sticks her cell phone in her purse. "She says Michael is going to contact Ranger Bob and let him know what we saw."

The image of Ranger Bob's shadow makes me wonder. What if . . .?

Dad chuckles. "Well, that should give him a good laugh. At the very least he can be on the lookout for some large animal that is apparently friends with Mortimer."

Lily unbuckles her seat belt. "Can I go over to Charlie's and get Muffin?"

Mom frowns. "That's 'May I' and yes, you may." Her cell phone rings again and she answers it. "Hi, Francine. Yes, we saw it, too. Now calm down . . ."

"I'll go with you," I say to Lily as I jump out of the car.

"Don't stay long," Dad yells after us. "I'm not unloading this whole van by myself."

Lily and I leap up the steps to Charlie's front porch and ring the doorbell. He answers the door holding Muffin. "Welcome home, you two!"

"Muffin!" Lily squeals as she takes her cat from Charlie's arms. "Did you miss me?" She strolls into the living room like it's her own house and sits on the floor with Muffin's toys.

Charlie chuckles and turns to me. "So how was the camping trip, my young Trailblazer? Did you see Bigfoot?"

My mouth drops open. "How do you know about Bigfoot?"

"Come, let me show you something." Charlie leads me to the living room couch. The coffee table in front of us is piled with scrapbooks, several open to pages crammed with photos.

"When your dad mentioned the campground you were going to, I had a feeling you might come home with all kinds of questions. I don't know if I have any answers, but I know your Grandpa would like me to share these pictures with you."

Charlie hands me a photo that shows two boys about my age, standing in front of a lake and each holding up a fish about a foot long. They both wear Minnesota Twins baseball caps and show off smiles as wide as their faces.

"That's your Grandpa and me,"

Charlie says. "We were about eight or nine years old there. We didn't have a group like the Trailblazers, but our dads would take us camping all the time. Our favorite spot was where you just spent the weekend."

"We caught some fish, too," I say. "Although, it really was Mortimer who caught all the fish. And we had a campfire with s'mores and Dad told scary stories."

"About Bigfoot?" Charlie asks.

I tilt my head and stare at Charlie. Like Grandpa, sometimes Charlie's eyes twinkle when he's teasing. But no eyes are twinkling now.

Charlie picks up another picture. "Here's something your Grandpa and I discovered on a hike near the lake."

I study the picture and gulp. A footprint, just like the one Justin and I found, stares back at me. I peer up at Charlie and open my mouth, but nothing comes out.

"Look familiar?"

I nod. "We found a footprint exactly like that." I reach in my pocket and pull out my camera. I scroll through the photos until I find the one I'm looking for. Holding it next to Charlie's picture, we can see it's an exact match.

Charlie gazes at the ceiling. His eyes look like they're somewhere far away. "So fifty years later, he still exists," he whispers.

I stare at the two photos, not knowing what to say. So Grandpa saw Bigfoot, too? He never mentioned anything about it. Maybe because he thought no one would believe him.

"Did you and Grandpa see Bigfoot?" My hand shakes as I hold the photo. "Was he as tall as the ceiling, with red hair all over his body, and smelled like rotten eggs?" Questions pour out of my mouth while Lily sits wide-eyed on the floor with Muffin purring in her lap.

Charlie chuckles. "We were never quite sure what we saw. We found some footprints and followed them to the edge of the lake where they disappeared. There were strands of red hair stuck to the bushes and this horrible smell, but we never actually saw anything alive. We didn't give up hope, though. Every time we went to that campground, we searched high and low for Bigfoot. Never found him. But it looks like maybe you and Mortimer solved the mystery."

I can't believe it. Was that really Bigfoot? Or Ranger Bob playing a joke on us? But Ranger Bob wasn't around fifty years ago to plant the footprints and red hair in exactly the same spots where we found them.

"I guess we'll just have to go camping there again sometime soon," I say. "Maybe you can come with us, Charlie."

"Maybe so, maybe so," Charlie says. "But you and I need to do something else first."

"What?" I study his face, looking for that twinkle in his eye.

Charlie grins. "Why, build a treehouse, of course!"

Kathie McMahon taught elementary school for 32 years, where she composed several school musicals. Kathie also collaborated on many youth theater musicals, receiving four ariZoni awards for Original Musical Composition. She is a member of SCBWI and has made presentations at several regional workshops. *Mortimer and Me: The Bigfoot Mystery* is the second book in the *Mortimer and Me* series. Kathie lives in Gilbert, Arizona, where you won't find any moose, but plenty of snakes, gila monsters, and mountain lions. For the latest news involving the adventures with Mortimer and Jimmy, visit her website at **www.kathiemcmahon.com**

TomTate is a graphic artist, cartoonist, woolgatherer and creator of *Mythles*, collections of 'Fairly' Tales that are more grin than Grimm. Drop in at **www.mythles.com** ... Hopefully, you'll 'leave happily ever after'!

Made in the USA
Coppell, TX
21 August 2021